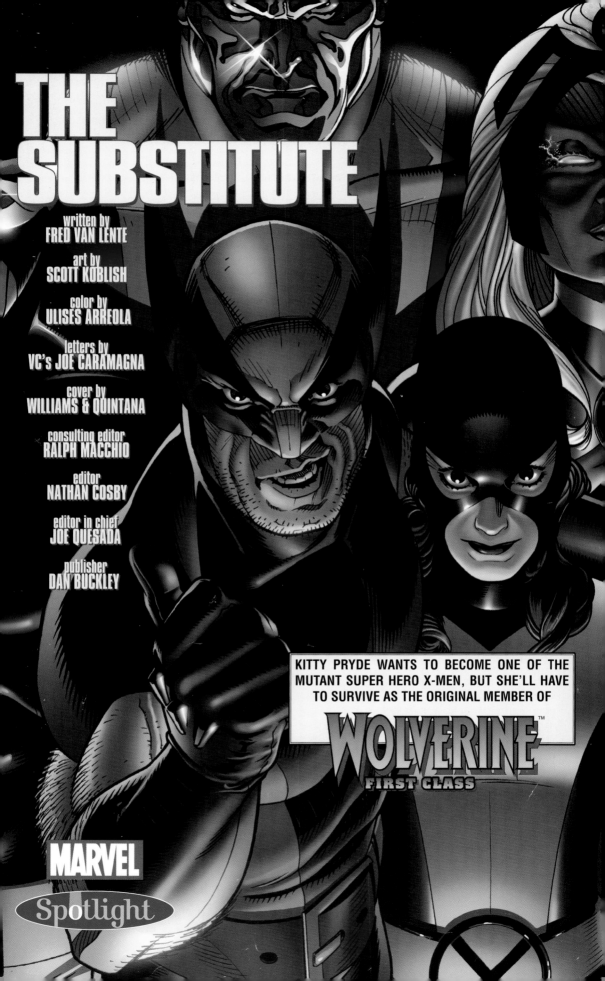

THE SUBSTITUTE

written by
FRED VAN LENTE

art by
SCOTT KOBLISH

color by
ULISES ARREOLA

letters by
VC's JOE CARAMAGNA

cover by
WILLIAMS & QUINTANA

consulting editor
RALPH MACCHIO

editor
NATHAN COSBY

editor in chief
JOE QUESADA

publisher
DAN BUCKLEY

KITTY PRYDE WANTS TO BECOME ONE OF THE
MUTANT SUPER HERO X-MEN, BUT SHE'LL HAVE
TO SURVIVE AS THE ORIGINAL MEMBER OF

WOLVERINE
FIRST CLASS

MARVEL

Spotlight

Visit us at www.abdopublishing.com

Reinforced library bound editions published in 2014 by Spotlight, a division of the
ABDO Group, PO Box 398166, Minneapolis, MN 55439. Spotlight produces
high-quality reinforced library bound editions for schools and libraries.
Published by agreement with Marvel Characters, Inc.

Printed in the United States of America, North Mankato, Minnesota.
042013
092013

♻ This book contains at least 10% recycled material.

marvel.com
© 2013 Marvel

Library of Congress Cataloging-in-Publication Data

Van Lente, Fred.
 The substitute / story by Fred Van Lente ; art by Scott Koblish. -- Reinforced library
bound edition.
     pages cm. -- (Wolverine, first class)
"Marvel."
 Summary: "Cyclops returns to the X-Men! Will Kitty Pryde continue her training
with him, or with Wolverine? Scott Summers and Logan duke it out over the right to
be her mentor!"-- Provided by publisher.
 ISBN 978-1-61479-181-2
1. Graphic novels. [1. Graphic novels. 2. Superheroes--Fiction.] I. Koblish, Scott,
illustrator. II. Title.
PZ7.7.V26Ss 2013
741.5'352--dc23
                                        2013005936

All Spotlight books are reinforced library bindings
and manufactured in the United States of America.

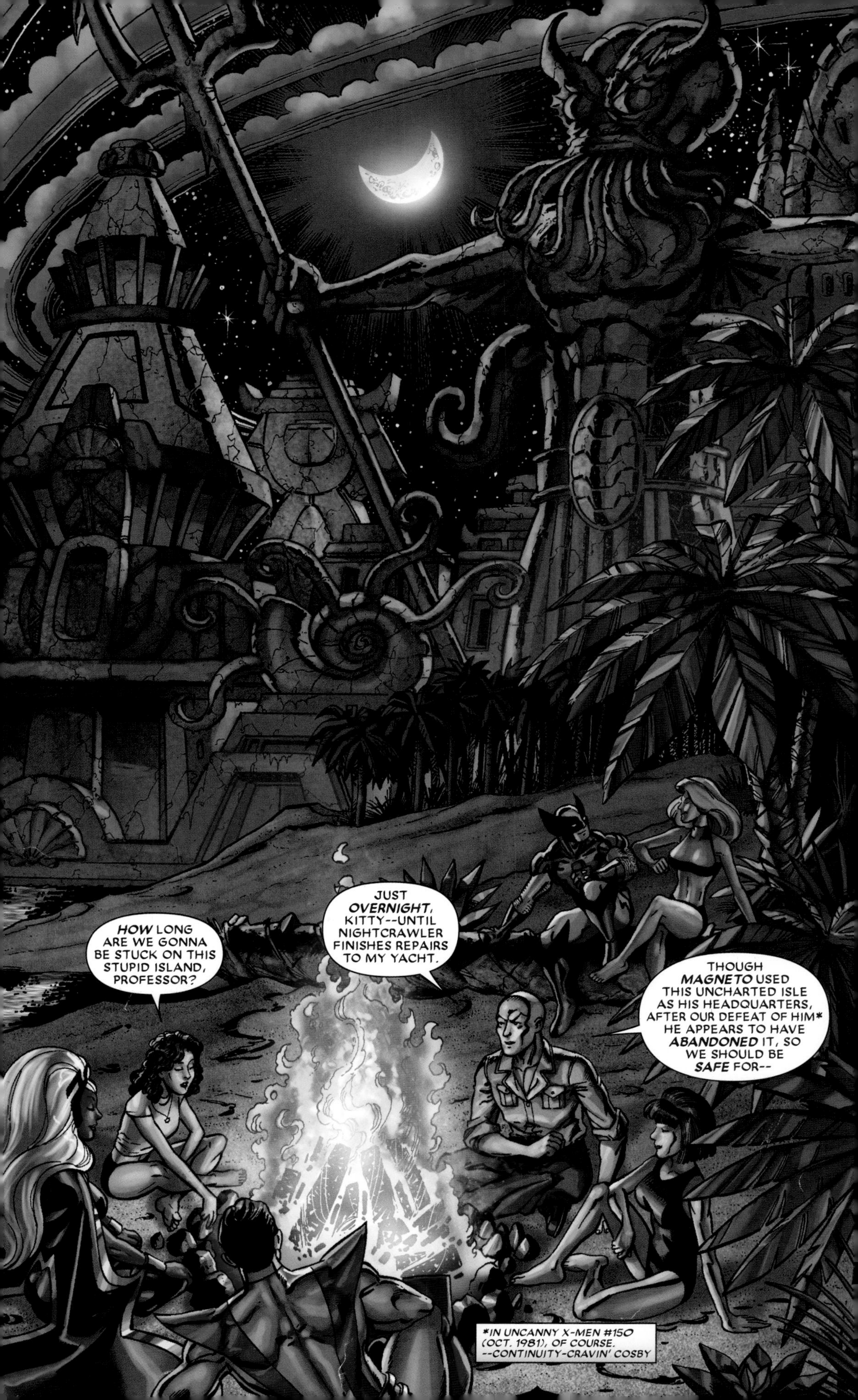
HOW LONG ARE WE GONNA BE STUCK ON THIS STUPID ISLAND, PROFESSOR?
JUST OVERNIGHT, KITTY--UNTIL NIGHTCRAWLER FINISHES REPAIRS TO MY YACHT.
THOUGH MAGNETO USED THIS UNCHARTED ISLE AS HIS HEADQUARTERS, AFTER OUR DEFEAT OF HIM* HE APPEARS TO HAVE ABANDONED IT, SO WE SHOULD BE SAFE FOR--
*IN UNCANNY X-MEN #150 (OCT. 1981), OF COURSE. --CONTINUITY-CRAVIN' COSBY

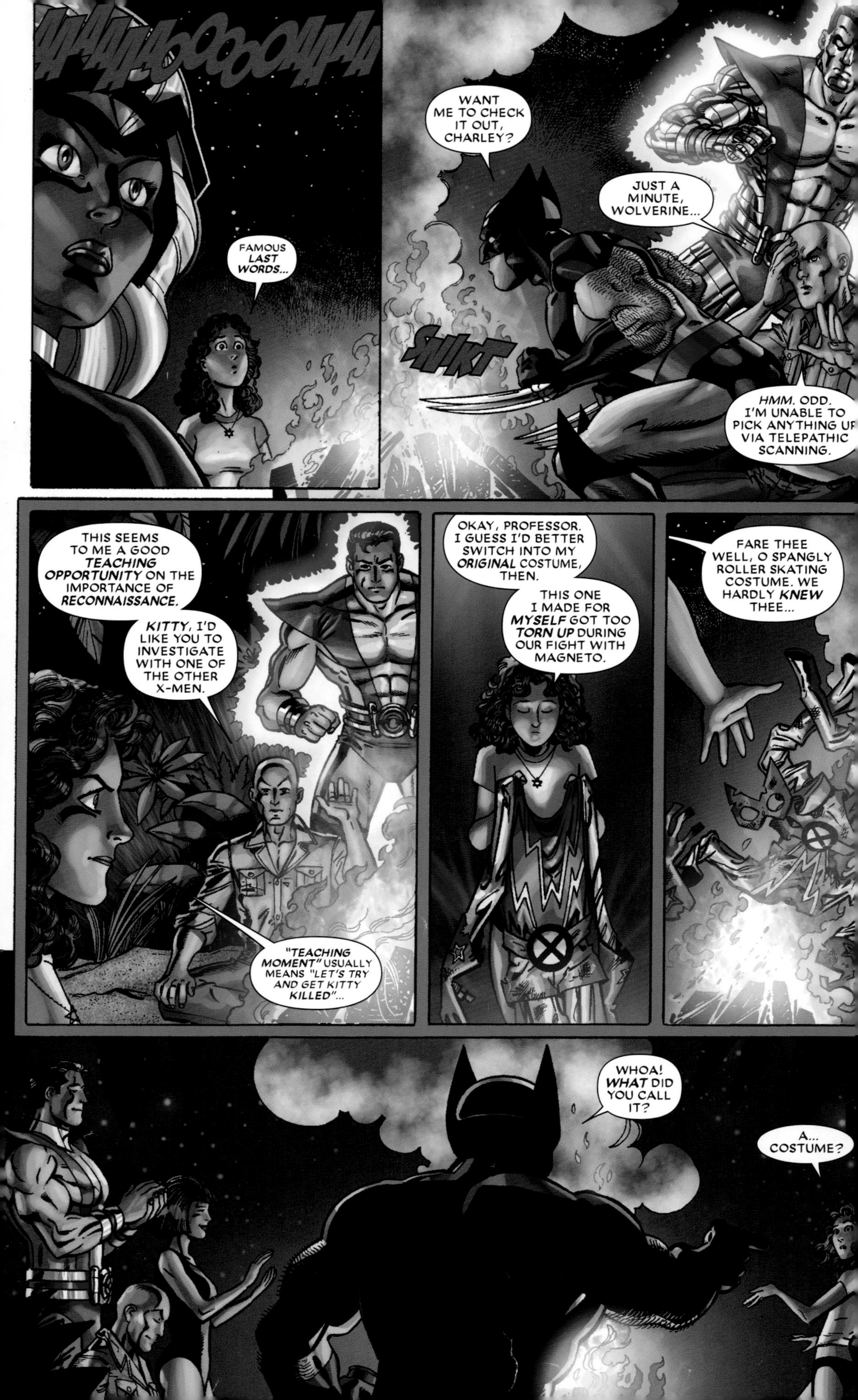
AAAAAOOOOOAAAA
FAMOUS LAST WORDS...
WANT ME TO CHECK IT OUT, CHARLEY?
JUST A MINUTE, WOLVERINE...
SNIKT
HMM. ODD. I'M UNABLE TO PICK ANYTHING UP VIA TELEPATHIC SCANNING.
THIS SEEMS TO ME A GOOD TEACHING OPPORTUNITY ON THE IMPORTANCE OF RECONNAISSANCE.
KITTY, I'D LIKE YOU TO INVESTIGATE WITH ONE OF THE OTHER X-MEN.
"TEACHING MOMENT" USUALLY MEANS "LET'S TRY AND GET KITTY KILLED"...
OKAY, PROFESSOR. I GUESS I'D BETTER SWITCH INTO MY ORIGINAL COSTUME, THEN.
THIS ONE I MADE FOR MYSELF GOT TOO TORN UP DURING OUR FIGHT WITH MAGNETO.
FARE THEE WELL, O SPANGLY ROLLER SKATING COSTUME. WE HARDLY KNEW THEE...
WHOA! WHAT DID YOU CALL IT?
A... COSTUME?

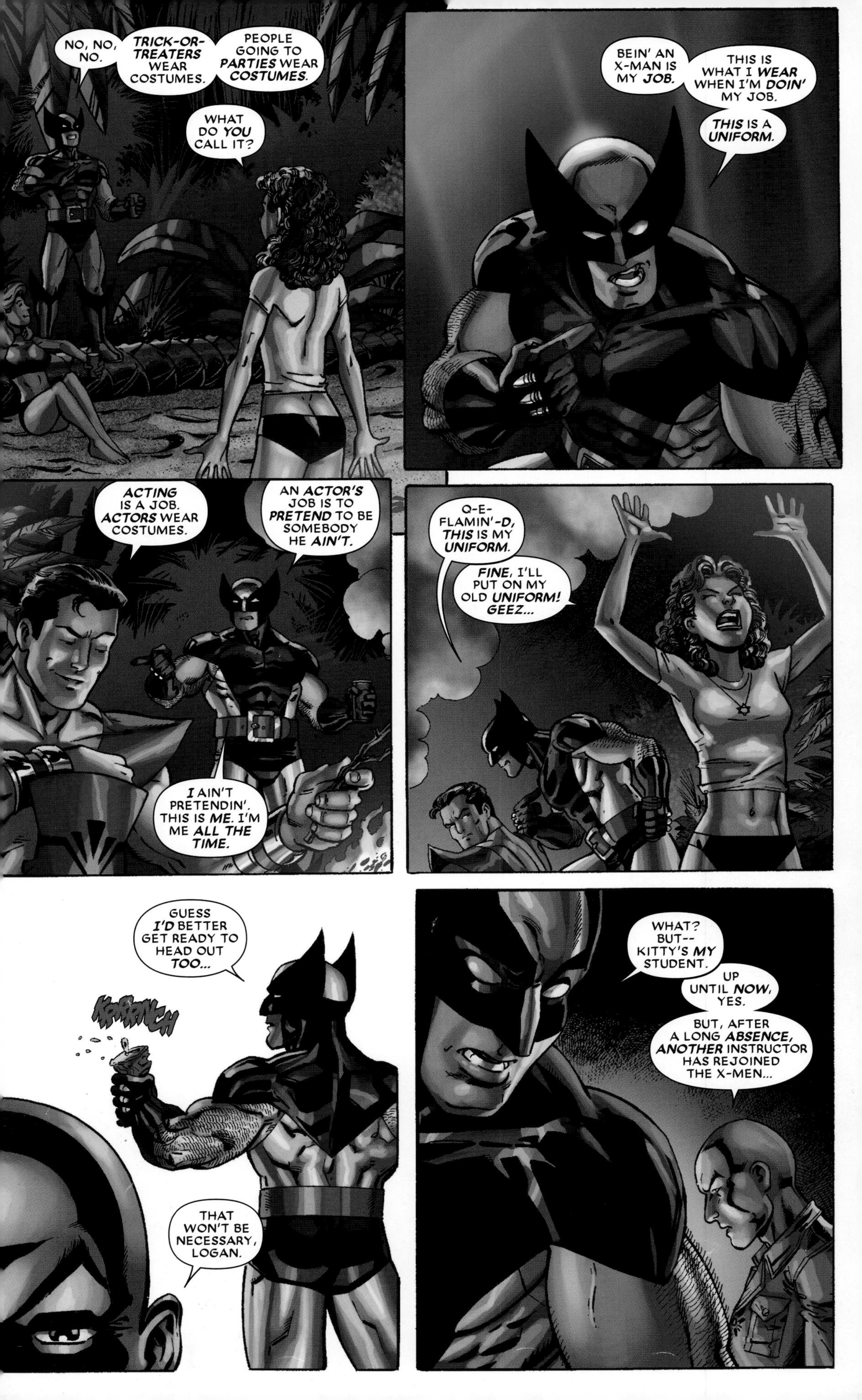
NO, NO, NO.
TRICK-OR-TREATERS WEAR COSTUMES.
PEOPLE GOING TO PARTIES WEAR COSTUMES.
WHAT DO YOU CALL IT?
BEIN' AN X-MAN IS MY JOB.
THIS IS WHAT I WEAR WHEN I'M DOIN' MY JOB.
THIS IS A UNIFORM.
ACTING IS A JOB. ACTORS WEAR COSTUMES.
AN ACTOR'S JOB IS TO PRETEND TO BE SOMEBODY HE AIN'T.
I AIN'T PRETENDIN'. THIS IS ME. I'M ME ALL THE TIME.
Q-E-FLAMIN'-D, THIS IS MY UNIFORM.
FINE, I'LL PUT ON MY OLD UNIFORM! GEEZ...
GUESS I'D BETTER GET READY TO HEAD OUT TOO...
KRRRNCH
THAT WON'T BE NECESSARY, LOGAN.
WHAT? BUT-- KITTY'S MY STUDENT.
UP UNTIL NOW, YES.
BUT, AFTER A LONG ABSENCE, ANOTHER INSTRUCTOR HAS REJOINED THE X-MEN...

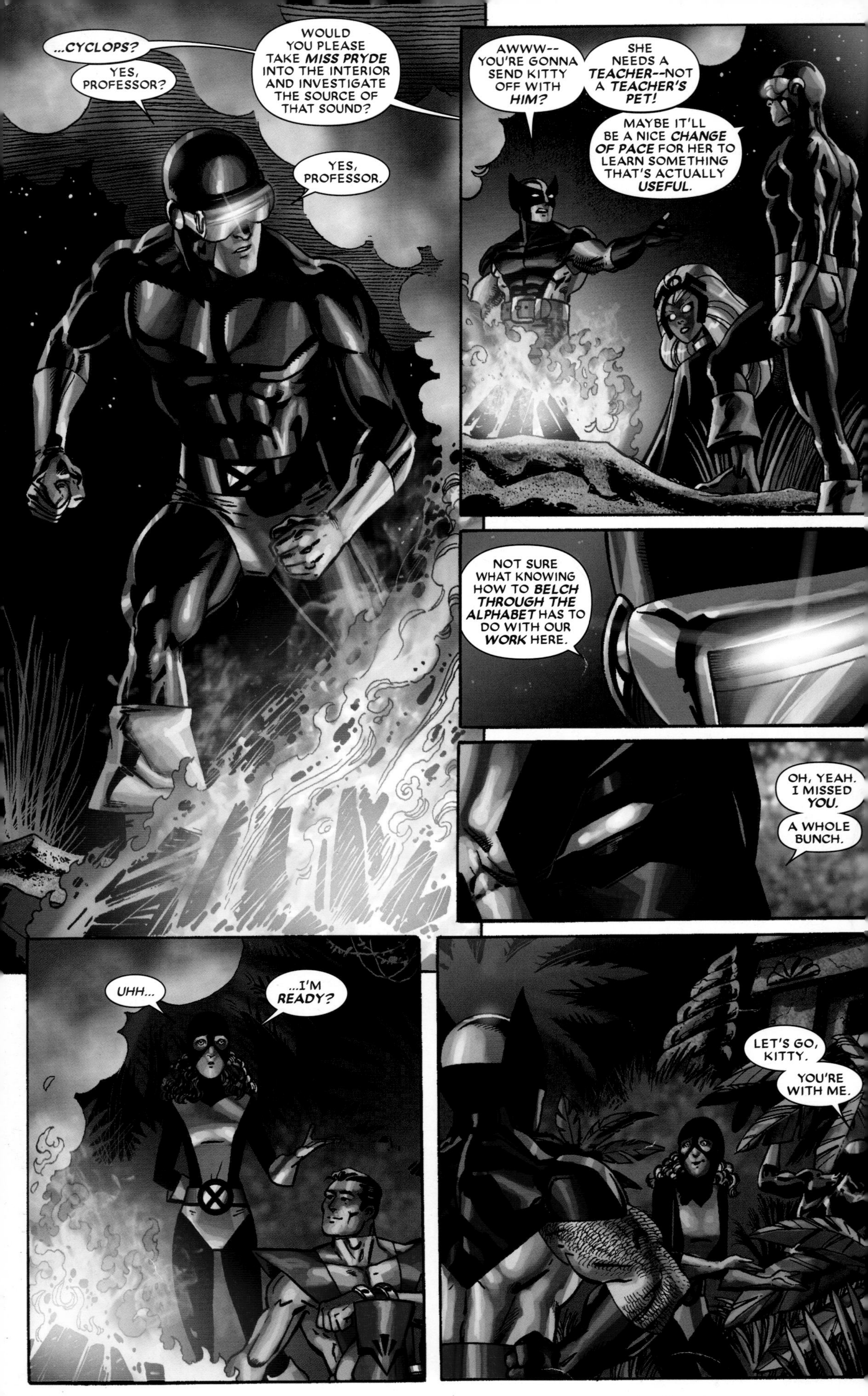

...CYCLOPS?
YES, PROFESSOR?
WOULD YOU PLEASE TAKE MISS PRYDE INTO THE INTERIOR AND INVESTIGATE THE SOURCE OF THAT SOUND?
YES, PROFESSOR.
AWWW-- YOU'RE GONNA SEND KITTY OFF WITH HIM?
SHE NEEDS A TEACHER--NOT A TEACHER'S PET!
MAYBE IT'LL BE A NICE CHANGE OF PACE FOR HER TO LEARN SOMETHING THAT'S ACTUALLY USEFUL.
NOT SURE WHAT KNOWING HOW TO BELCH THROUGH THE ALPHABET HAS TO DO WITH OUR WORK HERE.
OH, YEAH. I MISSED YOU.
A WHOLE BUNCH.
UHH...
...I'M READY?
LET'S GO, KITTY.
YOU'RE WITH ME.

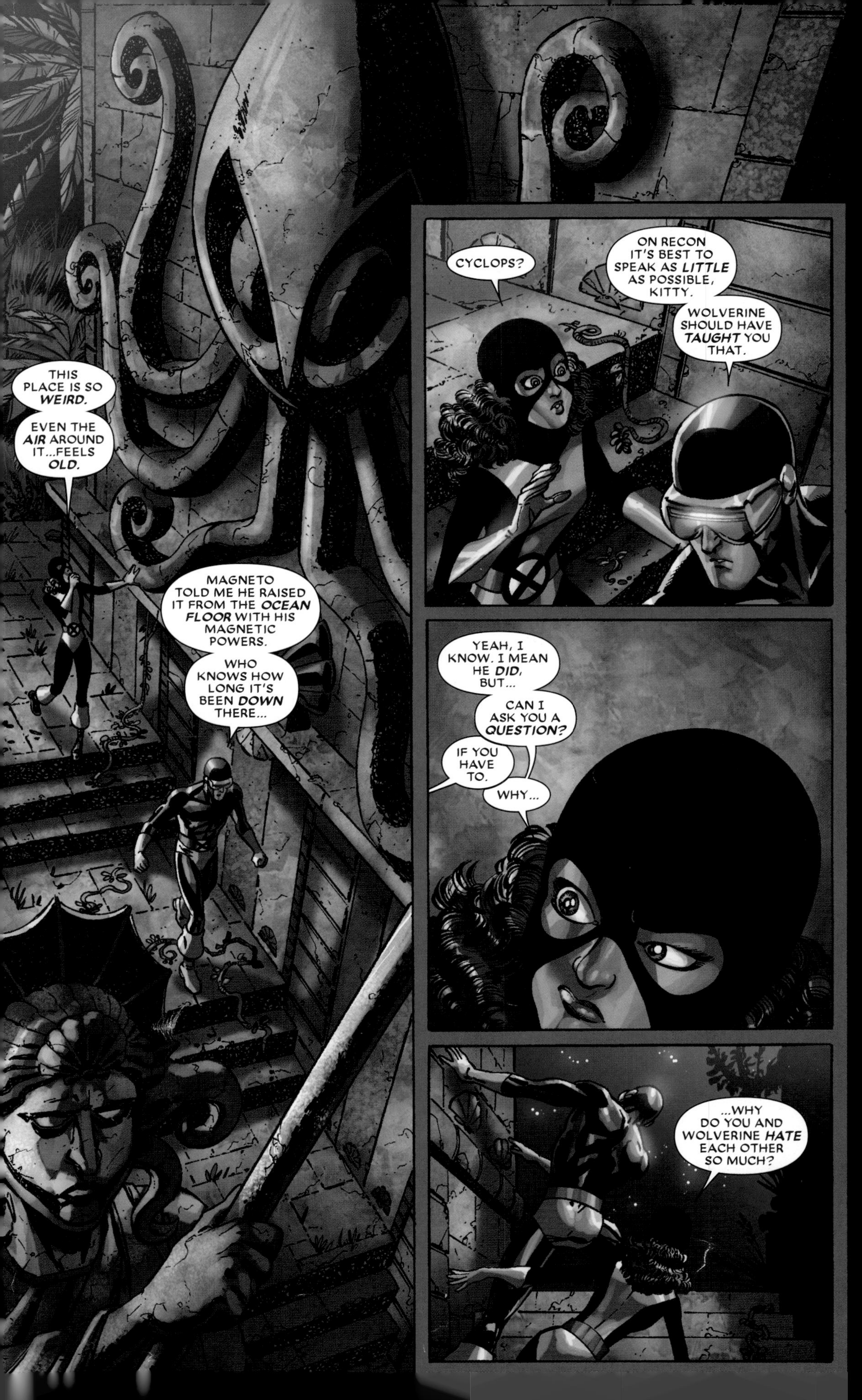
THIS PLACE IS SO WEIRD.
EVEN THE AIR AROUND IT...FEELS OLD.
MAGNETO TOLD ME HE RAISED IT FROM THE OCEAN FLOOR WITH HIS MAGNETIC POWERS.
WHO KNOWS HOW LONG IT'S BEEN DOWN THERE...
CYCLOPS?
ON RECON IT'S BEST TO SPEAK AS LITTLE AS POSSIBLE, KITTY.
WOLVERINE SHOULD HAVE TAUGHT YOU THAT.
YEAH, I KNOW. I MEAN HE DID, BUT...
CAN I ASK YOU A QUESTION?
IF YOU HAVE TO.
WHY...
...WHY DO YOU AND WOLVERINE HATE EACH OTHER SO MUCH?

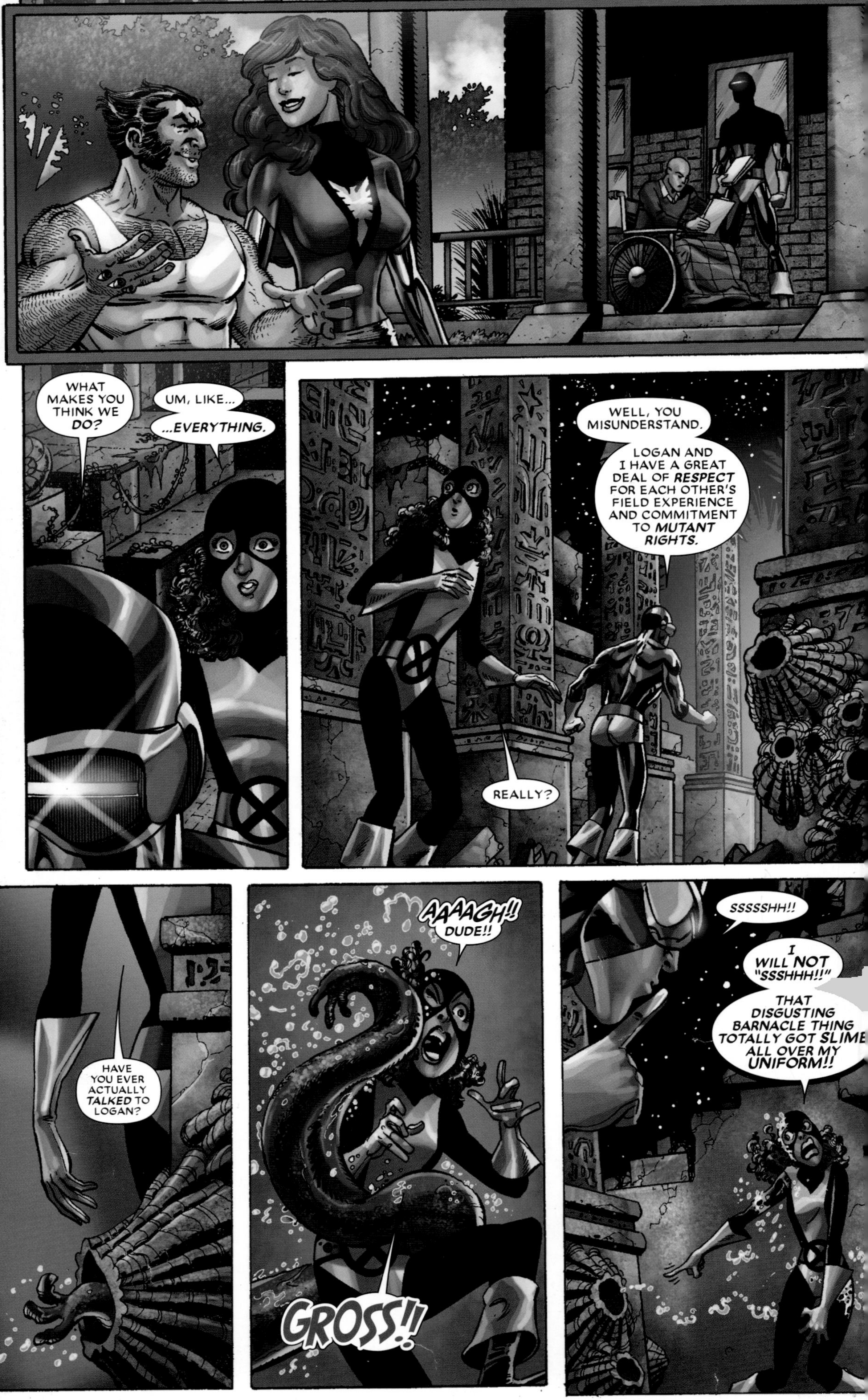
WHAT MAKES YOU THINK WE DO?
UM, LIKE...
...EVERYTHING.
WELL, YOU MISUNDERSTAND.
LOGAN AND I HAVE A GREAT DEAL OF RESPECT FOR EACH OTHER'S FIELD EXPERIENCE AND COMMITMENT TO MUTANT RIGHTS.
REALLY?
HAVE YOU EVER ACTUALLY TALKED TO LOGAN?
AAAAGH!! DUDE!!
GROSS!!
SSSSSHH!!
I WILL NOT "SSSHHH!!"
THAT DISGUSTING BARNACLE THING TOTALLY GOT SLIME ALL OVER MY UNIFORM!!

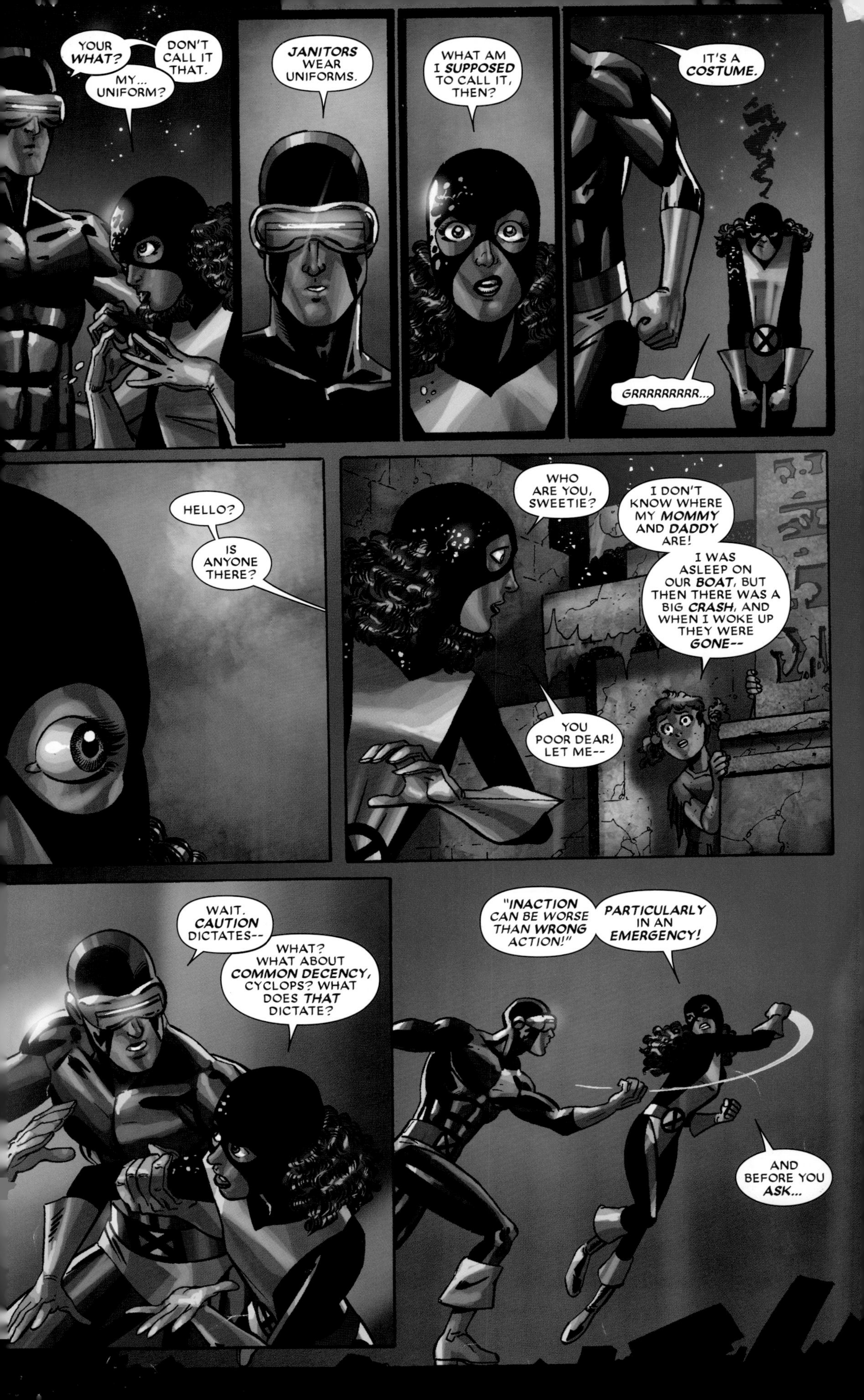

YOUR WHAT?
DON'T CALL IT THAT.
MY... UNIFORM?
JANITORS WEAR UNIFORMS.
WHAT AM I SUPPOSED TO CALL IT, THEN?
IT'S A COSTUME.
GRRRRRRRRR...
HELLO?
IS ANYONE THERE?
WHO ARE YOU, SWEETIE?
I DON'T KNOW WHERE MY MOMMY AND DADDY ARE!
I WAS ASLEEP ON OUR BOAT, BUT THEN THERE WAS A BIG CRASH, AND WHEN I WOKE UP THEY WERE GONE--
YOU POOR DEAR! LET ME--
WAIT. CAUTION DICTATES--
WHAT? WHAT ABOUT COMMON DECENCY, CYCLOPS? WHAT DOES THAT DICTATE?
"INACTION CAN BE WORSE THAN WRONG ACTION!"
PARTICULARLY IN AN EMERGENCY!
AND BEFORE YOU ASK...

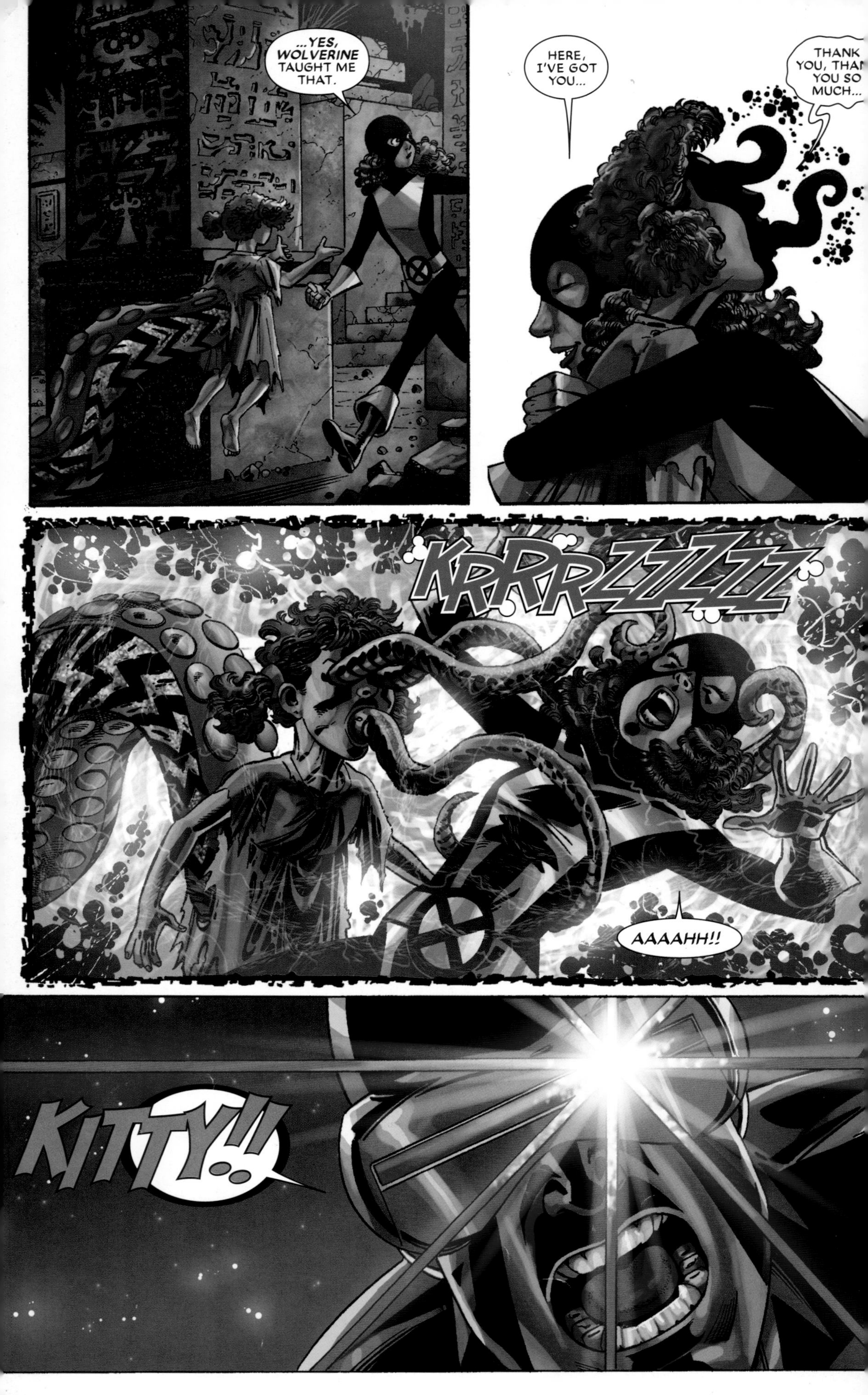
...YES, WOLVERINE TAUGHT ME THAT.
HERE, I'VE GOT YOU...
THANK YOU, THAN YOU SO MUCH...
KRRRRZZZZZ
AAAAHH!!
KITTY!!

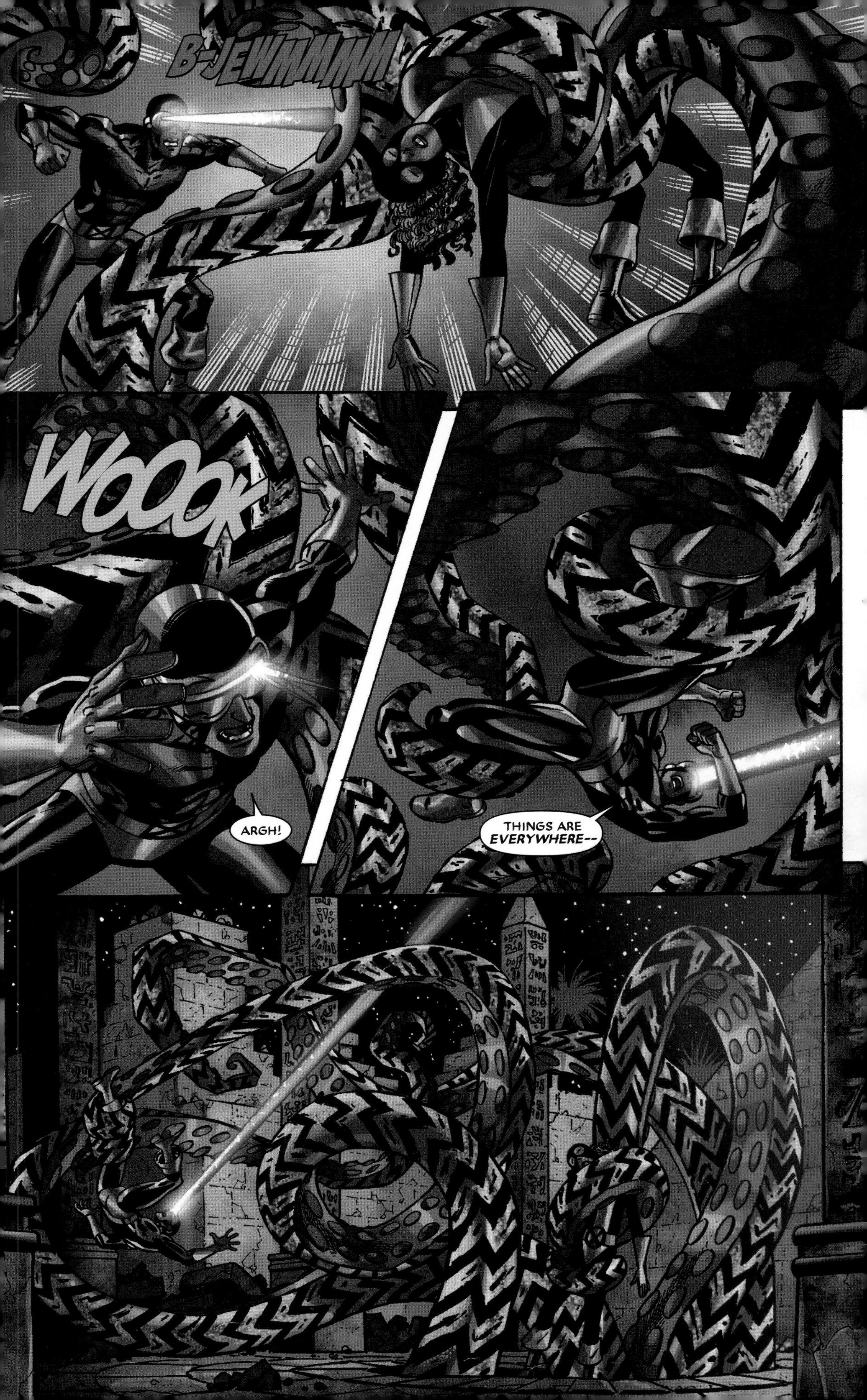

B-JEWMMMMM
WOOOK
ARGH!
THINGS ARE EVERYWHERE--

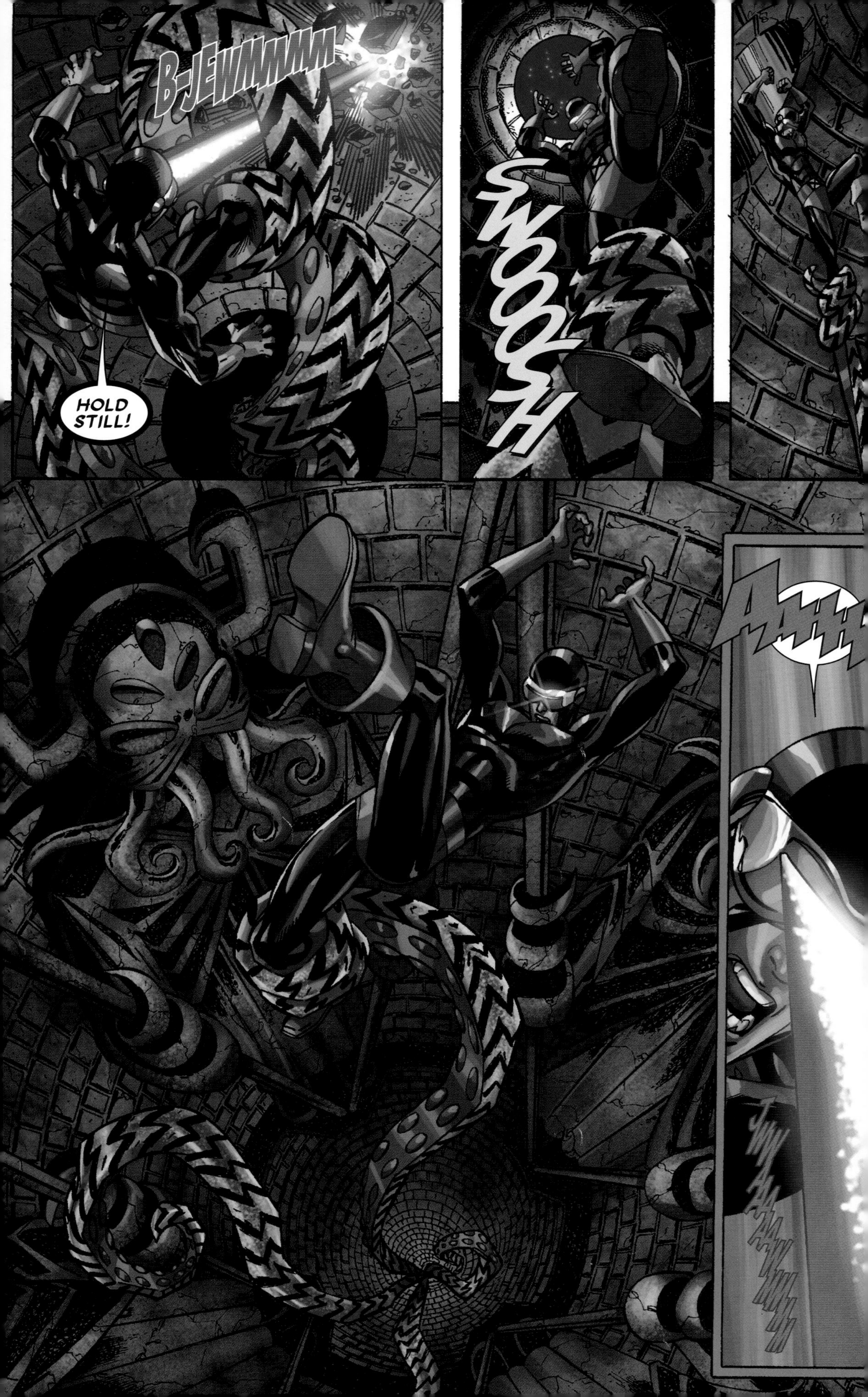
B-JEWMMMMM
HOLD STILL!
SWOOOSH

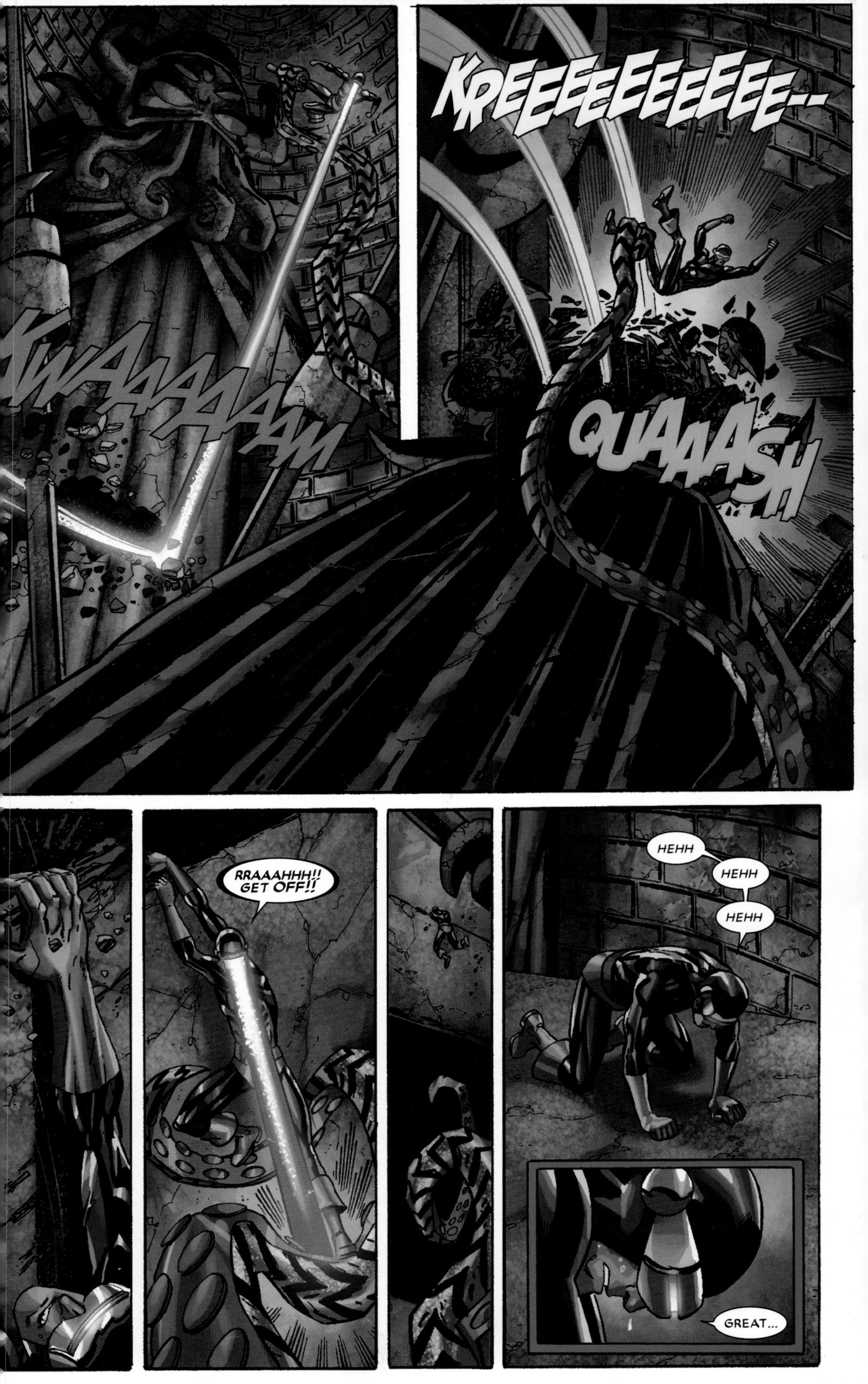

WAAAAAAM
KREEEEEEEEEE--
QUAAASH
RRAAAHHH!! GET OFF!!
HEHH
HEHH
HEHH
GREAT...

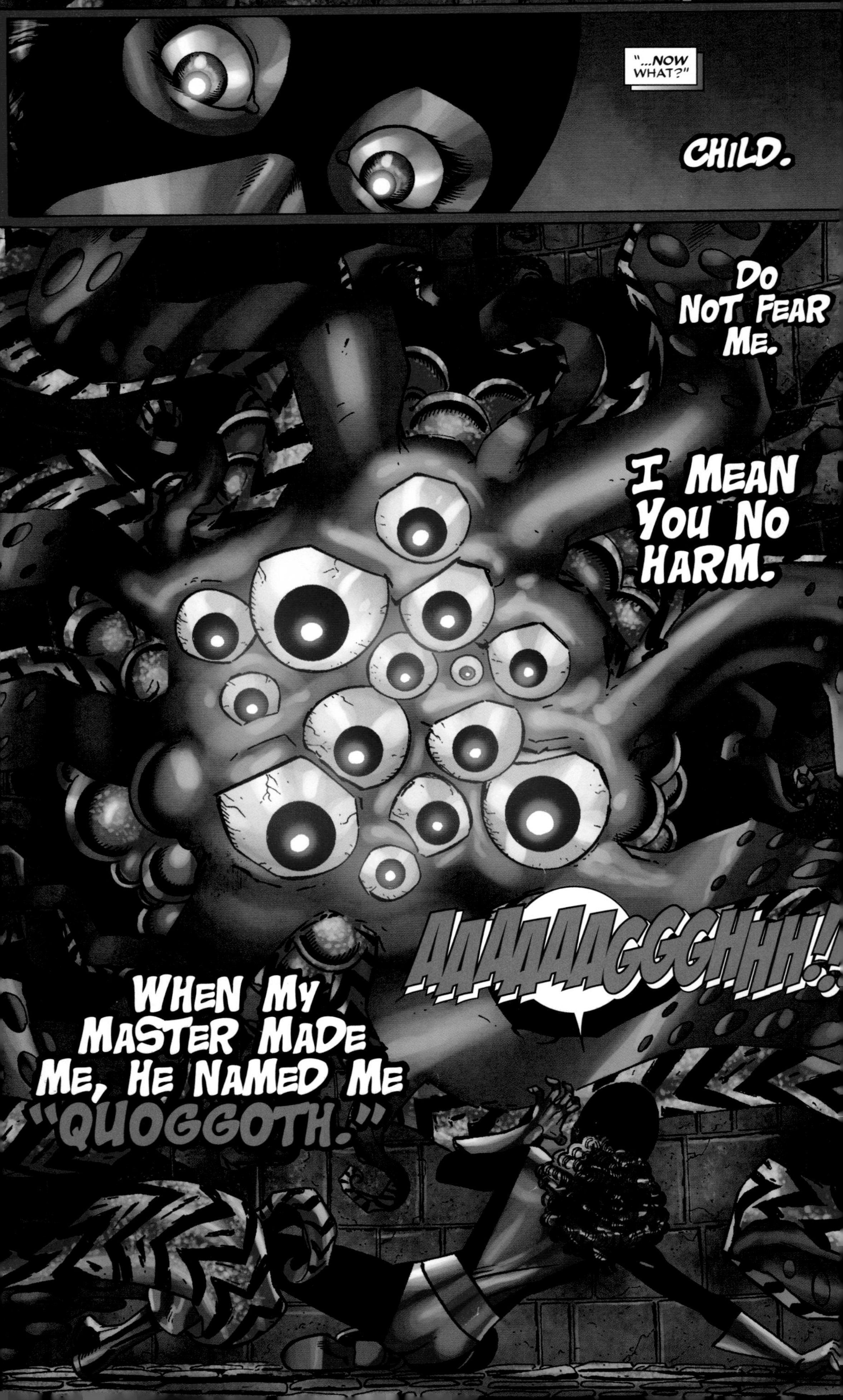
"...NOW WHAT?"
CHILD.
DO NOT FEAR ME.
I MEAN YOU NO HARM.
AAAAAAGGGHHH!!
WHEN MY MASTER MADE ME, HE NAMED ME "QUOGGOTH."

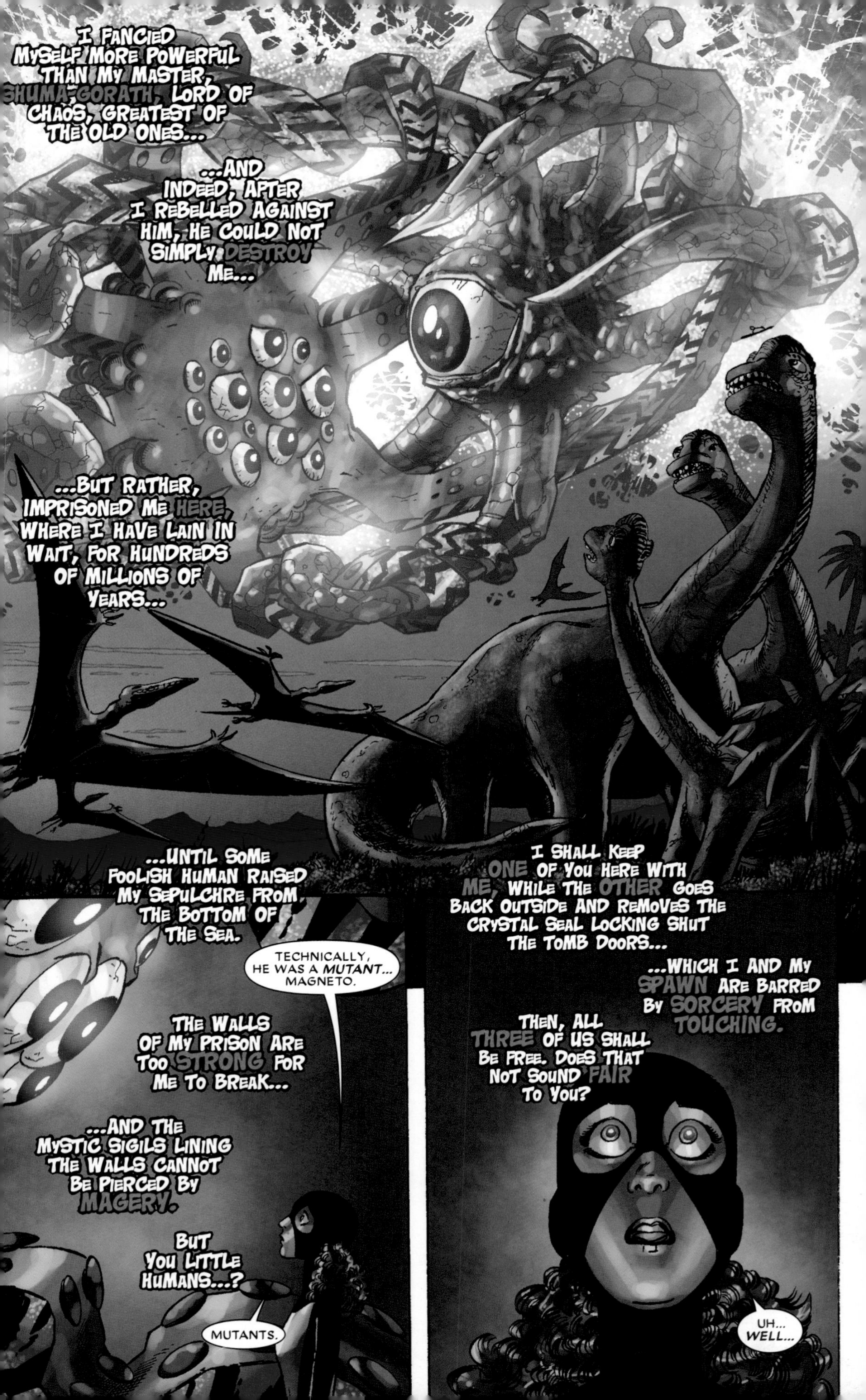
I FANCIED MYSELF MORE POWERFUL THAN MY MASTER, SHUMA-GORATH, LORD OF CHAOS, GREATEST OF THE OLD ONES...
...AND INDEED, AFTER I REBELLED AGAINST HIM, HE COULD NOT SIMPLY DESTROY ME...
...BUT RATHER, IMPRISONED ME HERE, WHERE I HAVE LAIN IN WAIT, FOR HUNDREDS OF MILLIONS OF YEARS...
...UNTIL SOME FOOLISH HUMAN RAISED MY SEPULCHRE FROM THE BOTTOM OF THE SEA.
TECHNICALLY, HE WAS A MUTANT... MAGNETO.
THE WALLS OF MY PRISON ARE TOO STRONG FOR ME TO BREAK...
...AND THE MYSTIC SIGILS LINING THE WALLS CANNOT BE PIERCED BY MAGERY.
BUT YOU LITTLE HUMANS...?
MUTANTS.
I SHALL KEEP ONE OF YOU HERE WITH ME, WHILE THE OTHER GOES BACK OUTSIDE AND REMOVES THE CRYSTAL SEAL LOCKING SHUT THE TOMB DOORS...
...WHICH I AND MY SPAWN ARE BARRED BY SORCERY FROM TOUCHING.
THEN, ALL THREE OF US SHALL BE FREE. DOES THAT NOT SOUND FAIR TO YOU?
UH... WELL...

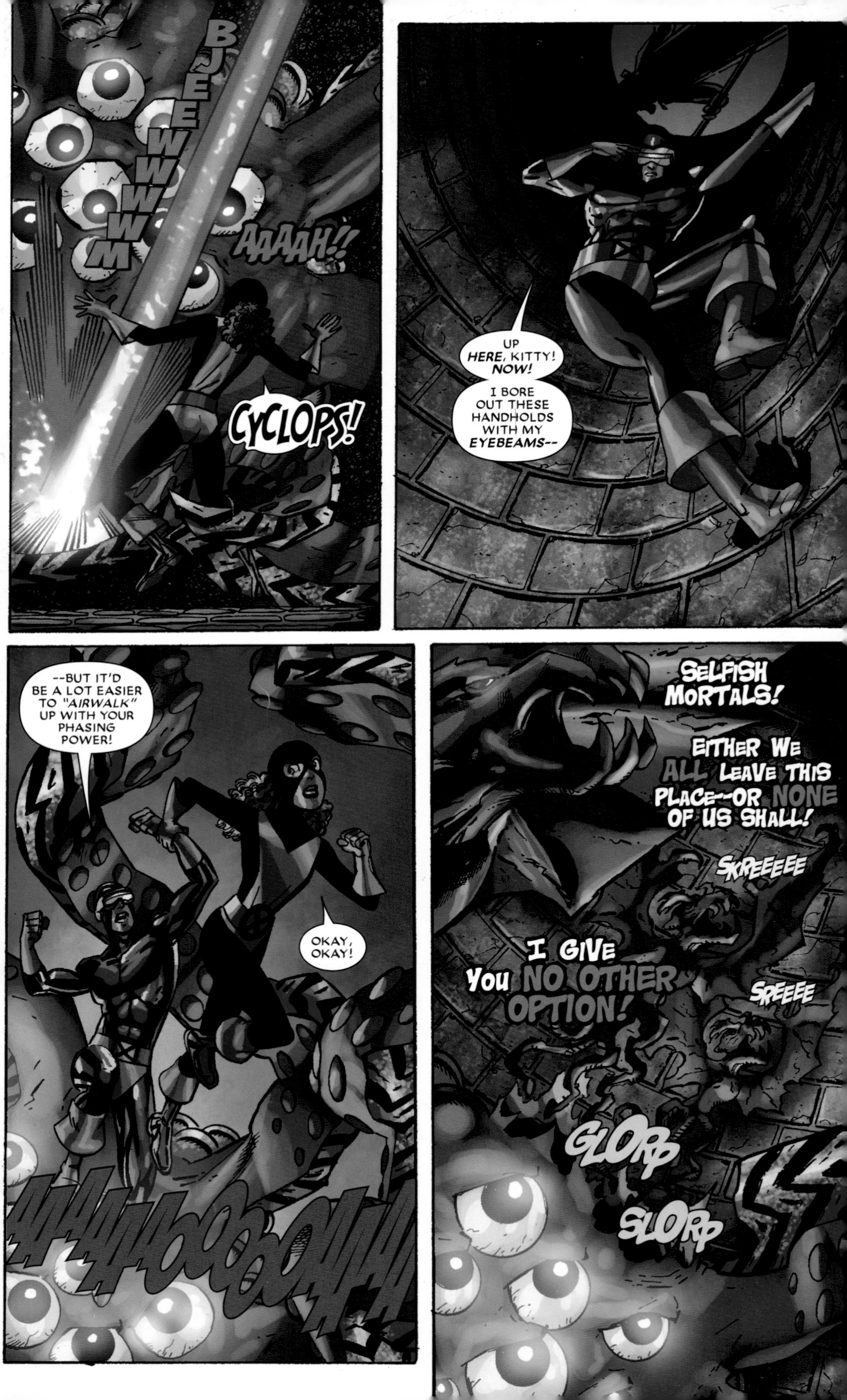
BJEEWWWWWM
AAAAH!!
CYCLOPS!
UP HERE, KITTY! NOW!
I BORE OUT THESE HANDHOLDS WITH MY EYEBEAMS--
--BUT IT'D BE A LOT EASIER TO "AIRWALK" UP WITH YOUR PHASING POWER!
OKAY, OKAY!
SELFISH MORTALS!
EITHER WE ALL LEAVE THIS PLACE--OR NONE OF US SHALL!
SKREEEEE
I GIVE YOU NO OTHER OPTION!
SREEEE
GLORP
SLORP

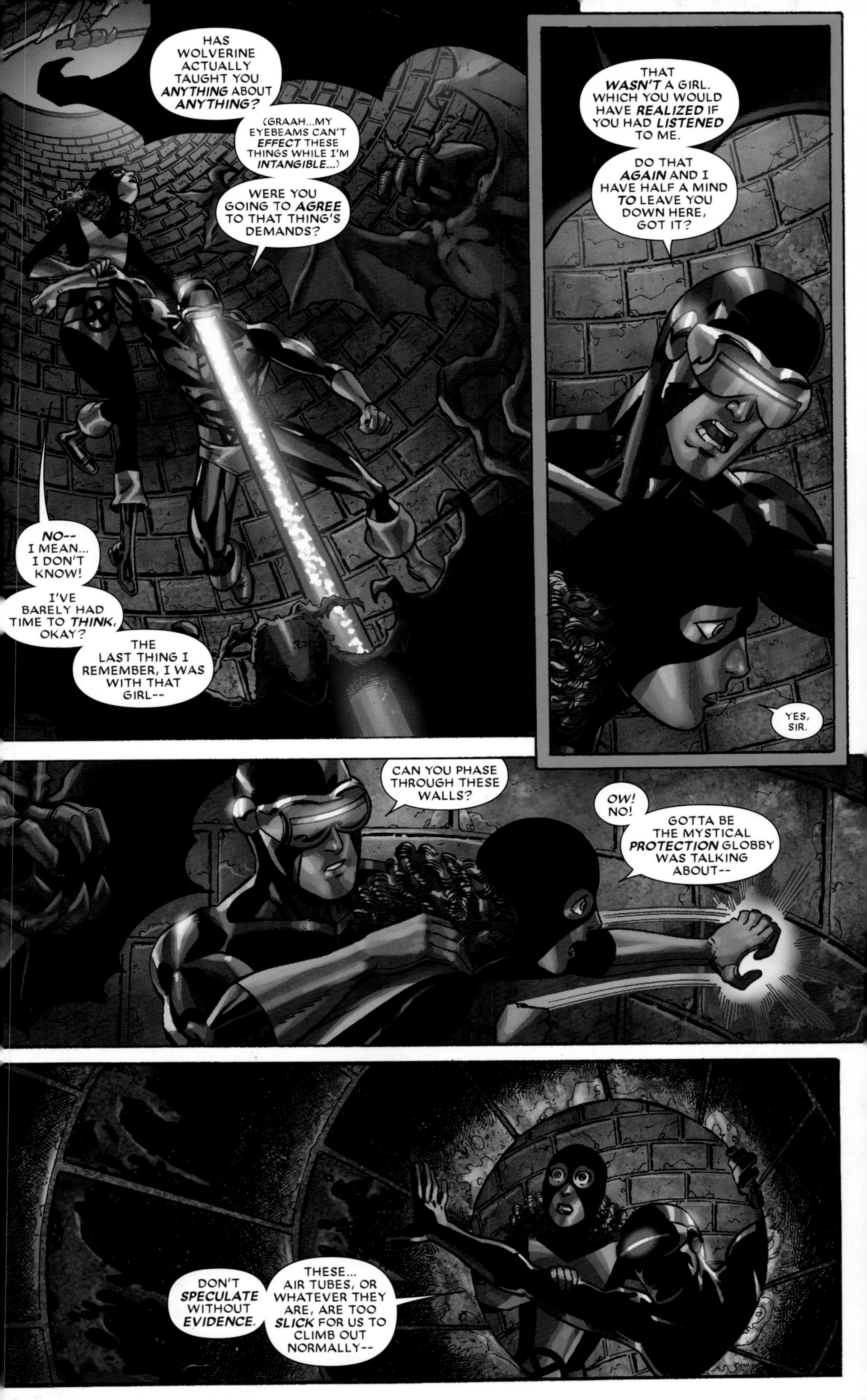
HAS WOLVERINE ACTUALLY TAUGHT YOU ANYTHING ABOUT ANYTHING?
(GRAAH...MY EYEBEAMS CAN'T EFFECT THESE THINGS WHILE I'M INTANGIBLE...)
WERE YOU GOING TO AGREE TO THAT THING'S DEMANDS?
NO-- I MEAN... I DON'T KNOW!
I'VE BARELY HAD TIME TO THINK, OKAY?
THE LAST THING I REMEMBER, I WAS WITH THAT GIRL--
THAT WASN'T A GIRL. WHICH YOU WOULD HAVE REALIZED IF YOU HAD LISTENED TO ME.
DO THAT AGAIN AND I HAVE HALF A MIND TO LEAVE YOU DOWN HERE, GOT IT?
YES, SIR.
CAN YOU PHASE THROUGH THESE WALLS?
OW! NO!
GOTTA BE THE MYSTICAL PROTECTION GLOBBY WAS TALKING ABOUT--
THESE... AIR TUBES, OR WHATEVER THEY ARE, ARE TOO SLICK FOR US TO CLIMB OUT NORMALLY--
DON'T SPECULATE WITHOUT EVIDENCE.

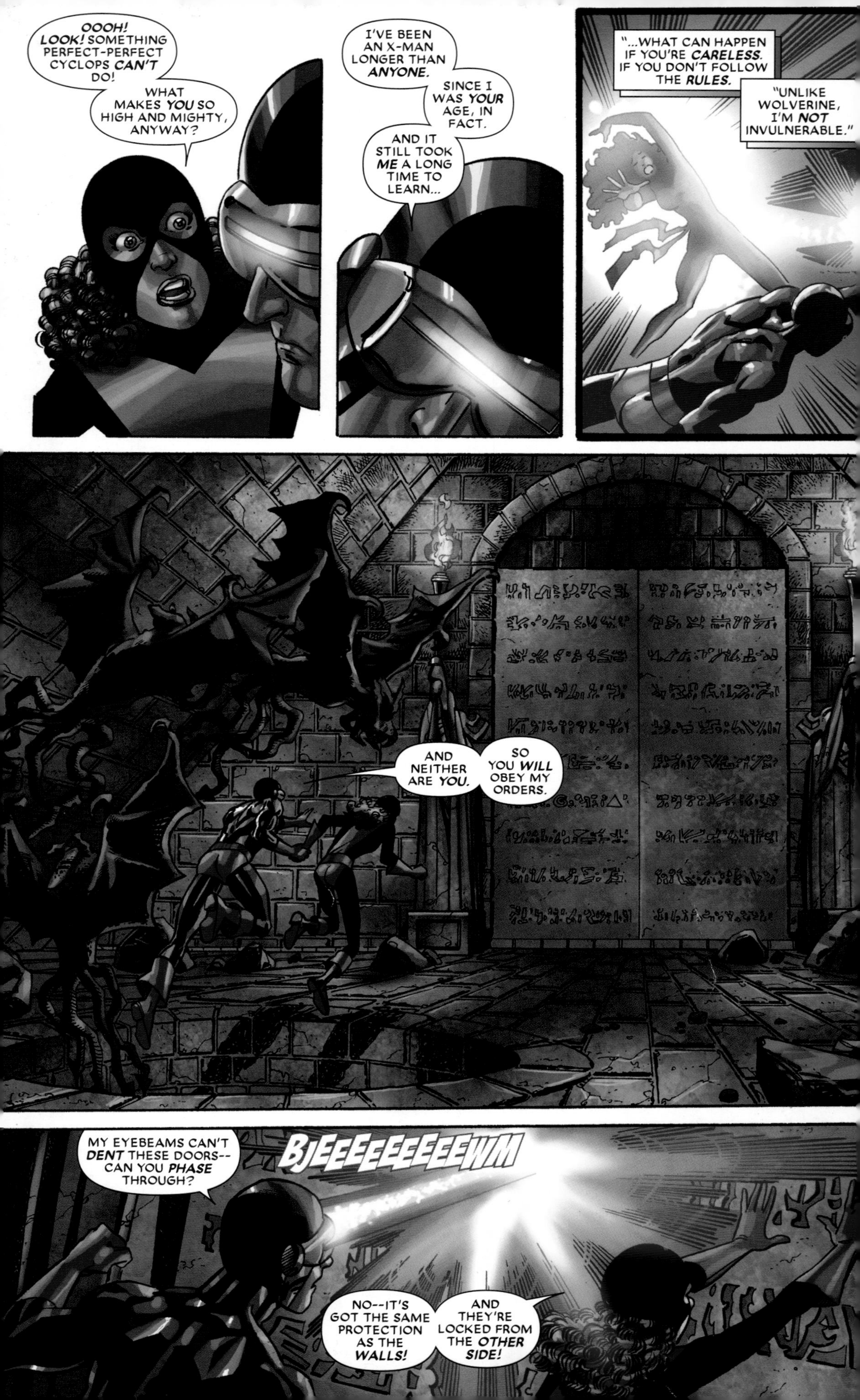
OOOH! LOOK! SOMETHING PERFECT-PERFECT CYCLOPS CAN'T DO!
WHAT MAKES YOU SO HIGH AND MIGHTY, ANYWAY?
I'VE BEEN AN X-MAN LONGER THAN ANYONE.
SINCE I WAS YOUR AGE, IN FACT.
AND IT STILL TOOK ME A LONG TIME TO LEARN...
"...WHAT CAN HAPPEN IF YOU'RE CARELESS. IF YOU DON'T FOLLOW THE RULES.
"UNLIKE WOLVERINE, I'M NOT INVULNERABLE."
AND NEITHER ARE YOU.
SO YOU WILL OBEY MY ORDERS.
MY EYEBEAMS CAN'T DENT THESE DOORS-- CAN YOU PHASE THROUGH?
BJEEEEEEEEEEWM
NO--IT'S GOT THE SAME PROTECTION AS THE WALLS!
AND THEY'RE LOCKED FROM THE OTHER SIDE!

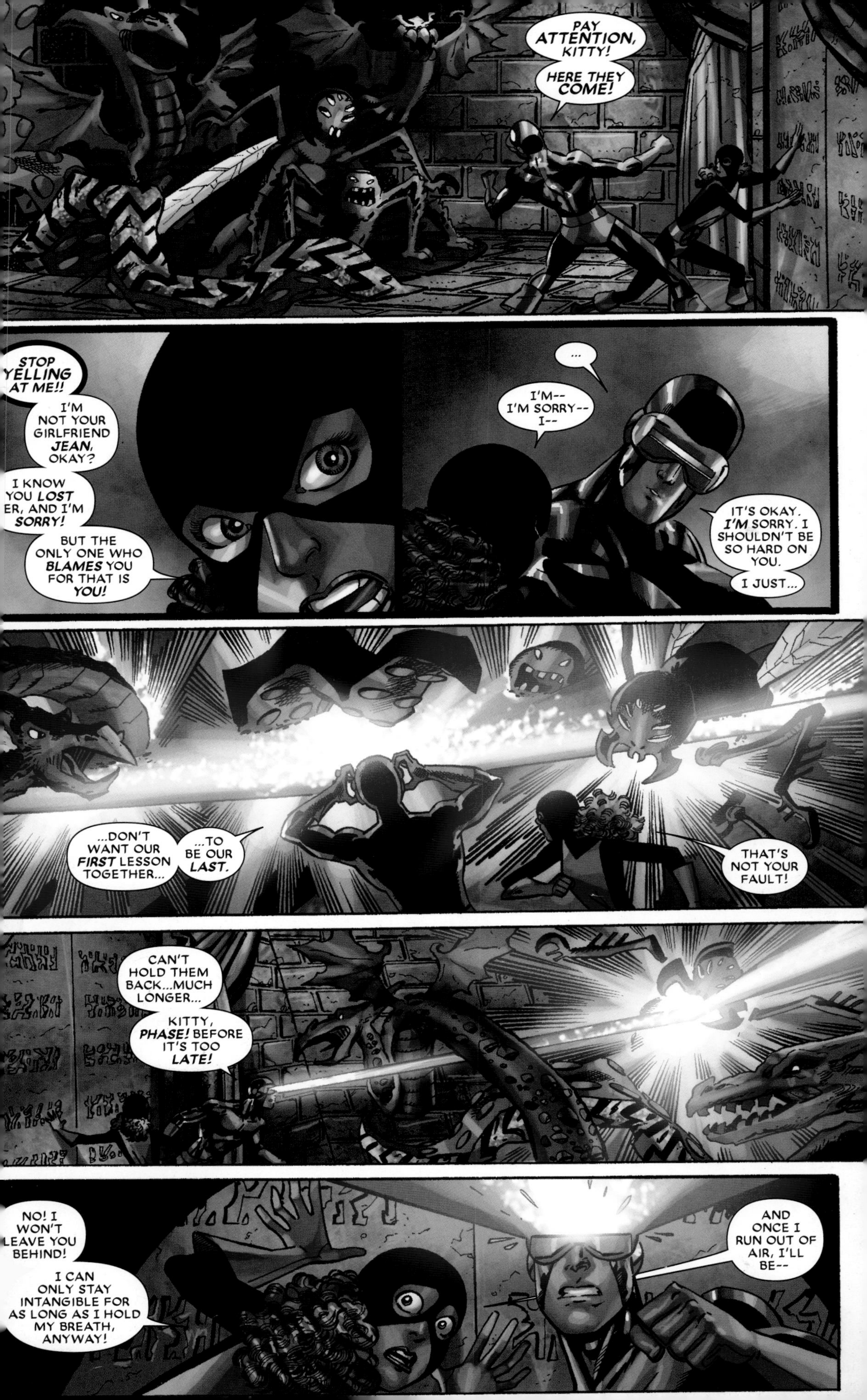
PAY ATTENTION, KITTY!
HERE THEY COME!
STOP YELLING AT ME!!
I'M NOT YOUR GIRLFRIEND JEAN, OKAY?
I KNOW YOU LOST ER, AND I'M SORRY!
BUT THE ONLY ONE WHO BLAMES YOU FOR THAT IS YOU!
...
I'M-- I'M SORRY-- I--
IT'S OKAY. I'M SORRY. I SHOULDN'T BE SO HARD ON YOU.
I JUST...
...DON'T WANT OUR FIRST LESSON TOGETHER...
...TO BE OUR LAST.
THAT'S NOT YOUR FAULT!
CAN'T HOLD THEM BACK...MUCH LONGER...
KITTY, PHASE! BEFORE IT'S TOO LATE!
NO! I WON'T LEAVE YOU BEHIND!
I CAN ONLY STAY INTANGIBLE FOR AS LONG AS I HOLD MY BREATH, ANYWAY!
AND ONCE I RUN OUT OF AIR, I'LL BE--

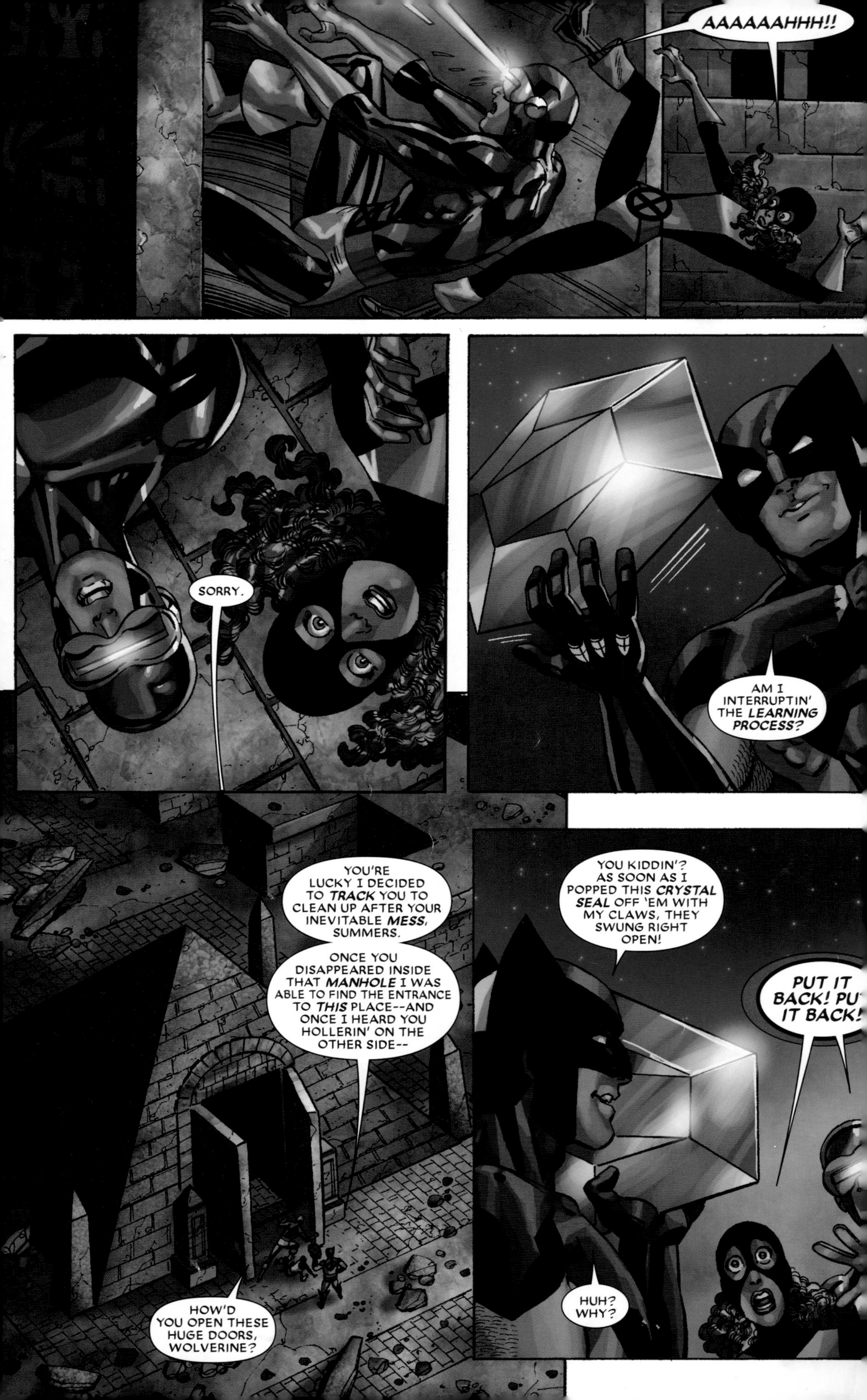
AAAAAAHHH!!
SORRY.
AM I INTERRUPTIN' THE LEARNING PROCESS?
YOU'RE LUCKY I DECIDED TO TRACK YOU TO CLEAN UP AFTER YOUR INEVITABLE MESS, SUMMERS.
ONCE YOU DISAPPEARED INSIDE THAT MANHOLE I WAS ABLE TO FIND THE ENTRANCE TO THIS PLACE--AND ONCE I HEARD YOU HOLLERIN' ON THE OTHER SIDE--
HOW'D YOU OPEN THESE HUGE DOORS, WOLVERINE?
YOU KIDDIN'? AS SOON AS I POPPED THIS CRYSTAL SEAL OFF 'EM WITH MY CLAWS, THEY SWUNG RIGHT OPEN!
PUT IT BACK! PUT IT BACK!
HUH? WHY?

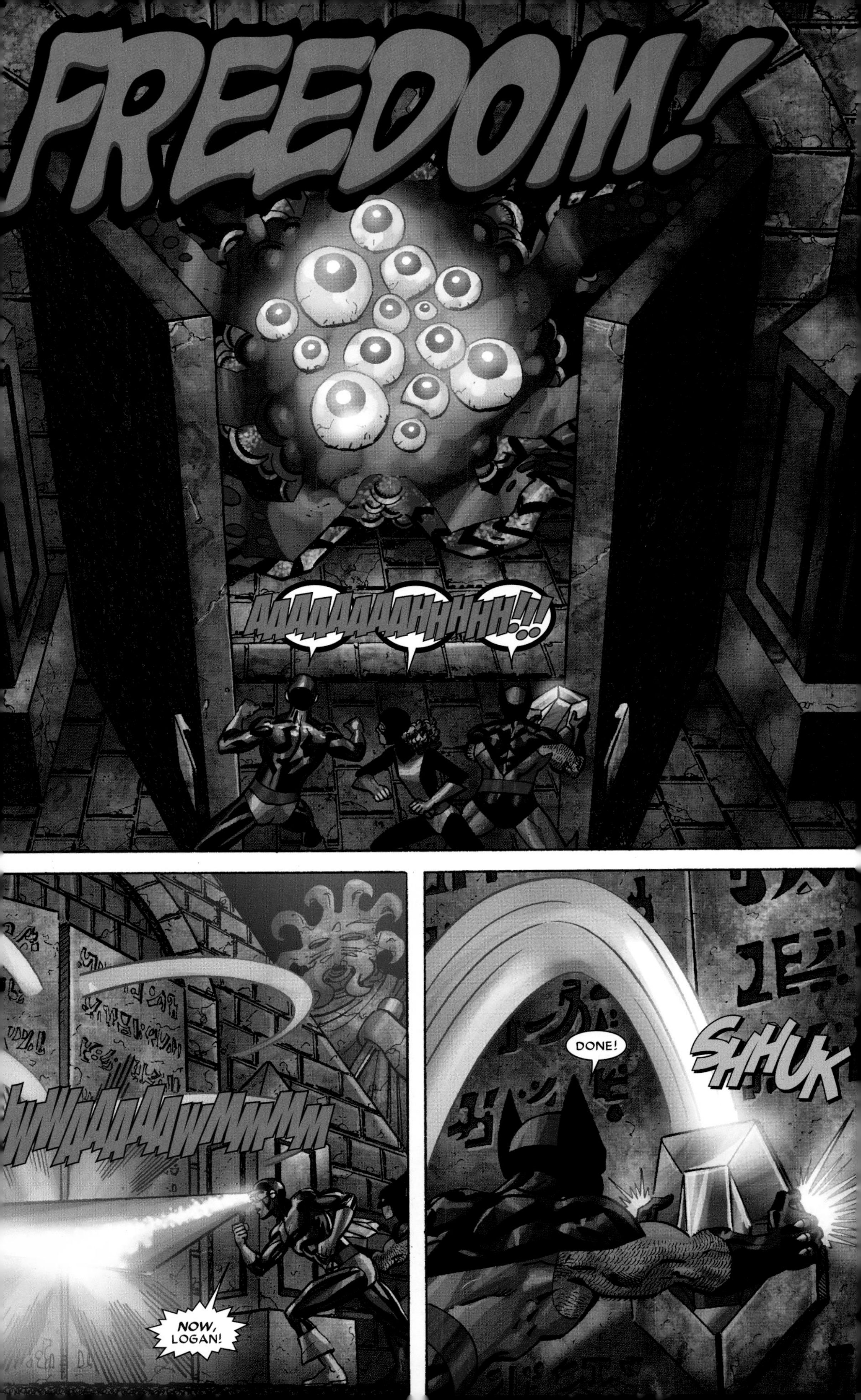

FREEDOM!
NOW, LOGAN!
DONE!
SHHUK

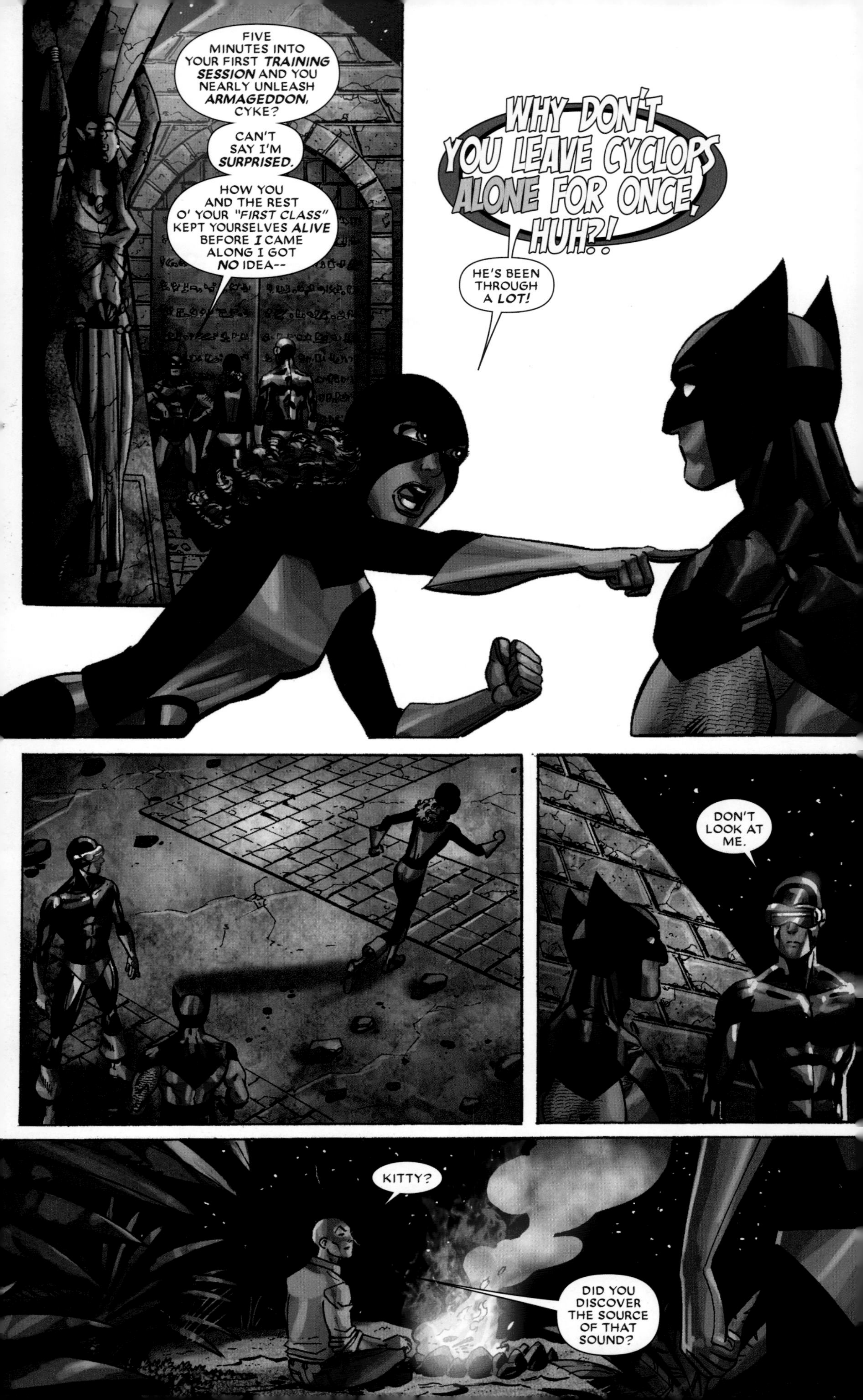
FIVE MINUTES INTO YOUR FIRST TRAINING SESSION AND YOU NEARLY UNLEASH ARMAGEDDON, CYKE?
CAN'T SAY I'M SURPRISED.
HOW YOU AND THE REST O' YOUR "FIRST CLASS" KEPT YOURSELVES ALIVE BEFORE I CAME ALONG I GOT NO IDEA--
WHY DON'T YOU LEAVE CYCLOPS ALONE FOR ONCE, HUH?!
HE'S BEEN THROUGH A LOT!
DON'T LOOK AT ME.
KITTY?
DID YOU DISCOVER THE SOURCE OF THAT SOUND?

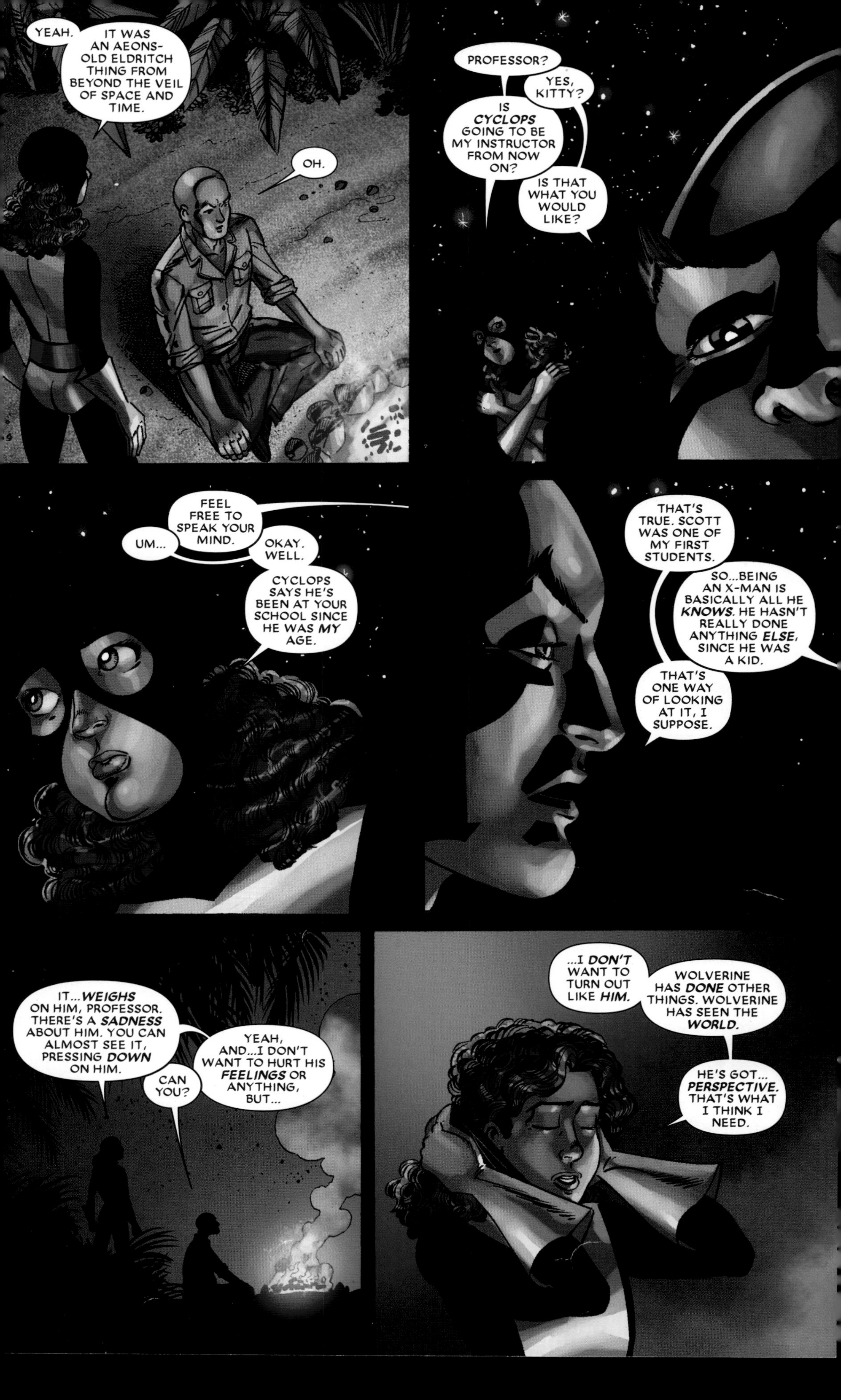
YEAH.
IT WAS AN AEONS-OLD ELDRITCH THING FROM BEYOND THE VEIL OF SPACE AND TIME.
OH.
PROFESSOR?
YES, KITTY?
IS *CYCLOPS* GOING TO BE MY INSTRUCTOR FROM NOW ON?
IS THAT WHAT YOU WOULD LIKE?
UM...
FEEL FREE TO SPEAK YOUR MIND.
OKAY. WELL.
CYCLOPS SAYS HE'S BEEN AT YOUR SCHOOL SINCE HE WAS *MY* AGE.
THAT'S TRUE. SCOTT WAS ONE OF MY FIRST STUDENTS.
SO...BEING AN X-MAN IS BASICALLY ALL HE *KNOWS*. HE HASN'T REALLY DONE ANYTHING *ELSE*, SINCE HE WAS A KID.
THAT'S ONE WAY OF LOOKING AT IT, I SUPPOSE.
IT...*WEIGHS* ON HIM, PROFESSOR. THERE'S A *SADNESS* ABOUT HIM. YOU CAN ALMOST SEE IT, PRESSING *DOWN* ON HIM.
CAN YOU?
YEAH, AND...I DON'T WANT TO HURT HIS *FEELINGS* OR ANYTHING, BUT...
...I *DON'T* WANT TO TURN OUT LIKE *HIM*.
WOLVERINE HAS *DONE* OTHER THINGS. WOLVERINE HAS SEEN THE *WORLD*.
HE'S GOT... *PERSPECTIVE*. THAT'S WHAT I THINK I NEED.

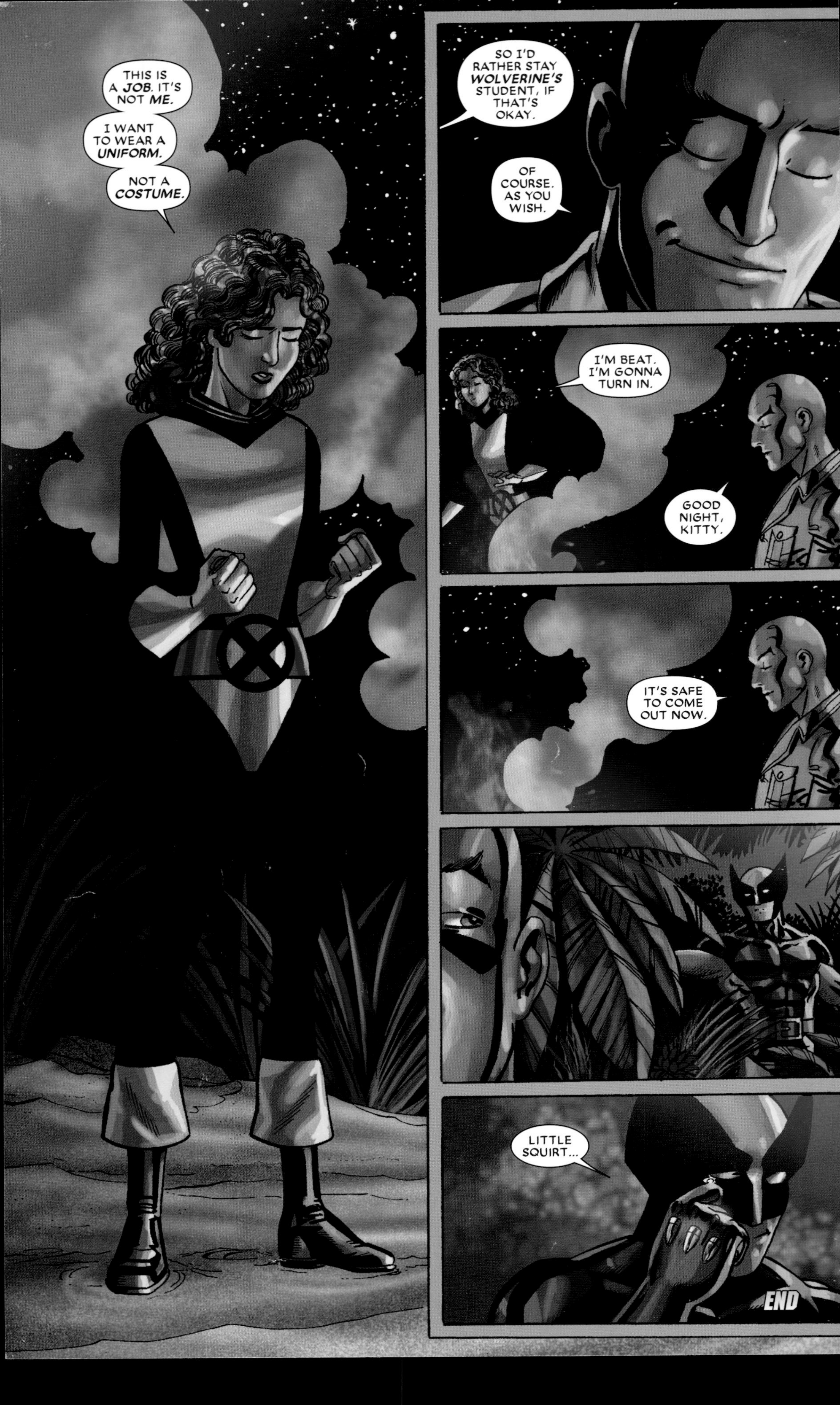
THIS IS A JOB. IT'S NOT ME.
I WANT TO WEAR A UNIFORM.
NOT A COSTUME.
SO I'D RATHER STAY WOLVERINE'S STUDENT, IF THAT'S OKAY.
OF COURSE. AS YOU WISH.
I'M BEAT. I'M GONNA TURN IN.
GOOD NIGHT, KITTY.
IT'S SAFE TO COME OUT NOW.
LITTLE SQUIRT...
END